GREAT EXPECTATIONS

CHARLES DICKENS

www.realreads.co.uk

Retold by Gill Tavner
Illustrated by Karen Donnelly

Published by Real Reads Ltd
Stroud, Gloucestershire, UK
www.realreads.co.uk

Text copyright © Gill Tavner 2007
Illustrations copyright © Karen Donnelly 2007
The right of Gill Tavner to be identified as author of this book
has been asserted by her in accordance with the
Copyright, Design and Patents Act 1988

First published in 2007
Reprinted 2010

ISBN 978-1-906230-01-2

Printed in China by Imago Ltd
Designed by Lucy Guenot
Typeset by Bookcraft Ltd, Stroud, Gloucestershire

CONTENTS

THE CHARACTERS

Pip
As Pip grows from a young boy into a young man, he wants answers to many questions. Will the answers surprise him? Can he soften Estella's heart?

Magwitch
A dangerous, desperate villain. Will he harm Pip, or help him?

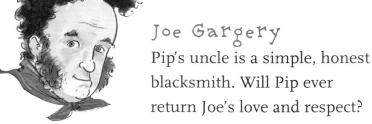

Joe Gargery
Pip's uncle is a simple, honest blacksmith. Will Pip ever return Joe's love and respect?

Mrs Gargery

Pip's angry, frightening sister. Will she ever discover the truth about her pork pie?

Estella

Cold, cruel and beautiful. Why does she want to break Pip's heart? Will she succeed?

Miss Havisham

A heart-broken and bitter old lady. Despite her strangeness, does she want to help Pip?

Biddy

An adorable village girl. Whose heart will she win?

GREAT EXPECTATIONS

A little bundle of shivers called Pip stood in front of his parents' gravestones, afraid and crying. The savage wind howling across the unfriendly marshes threw the dark mist at him, making him cry even louder.

'Hold yer noise!' roared a terrible voice. A man appeared between the graves and put his hand roughly over Pip's mouth. 'Keep still, you little devil, or I'll cut yer throat.'

He was a large man in rough grey clothes. On one leg was a prisoner's heavy leg iron, which made him limp. He wore an old rag around his head, and his shoes were broken. He was soaked, smothered in mud, stung, torn and cut. He shivered and glared at Pip, then growled, 'Tell us yer name. Quick! Show us where you live, you young dog.'

He tipped the terrified Pip upside down to empty his pockets, making it impossible for

Pip to work out where he did live. 'What fat cheeks you ha' got,' he told Pip's upside-down face. 'Darn me if I couldn't eat 'em.'

He turned Pip back onto his feet. 'Tomorrow you get me a file to cut off this leg iron, and some food, or I'll 'ave yer 'eart and liver fer me breakfast. And you do it secretly, or I'll creep into yer home when you're all comfy and safe and warm in bed, and I'll tear you open.'

His great hands at last released Pip. Not once looking back, Pip ran all the way home.

For the rest of that evening Pip felt terrified. At suppertime he managed to sneak some bread and cheese into his lap without anyone noticing. After supper he crept into the kitchen and gathered together half a jar of mincemeat, an old bone with a little meat still on it, and some brandy. Then he noticed a whole perfect pork pie on the shelf, and took that too. Finally, still unnoticed, he crept into the workshop and found a file.

Very early the next damp, dreary, misty morning, Pip once more set off into the marshes. The wind lashed at him and the mist made it hard to see. As he ran, stumbling, he imagined that he was being chased by a horde of people shouting 'Stop thief! Stop that boy! He's stolen a perfect pork pie!'

Little Pip was panting and trembling when the shape of the man loomed out of the mist ahead. Though he was still a frightening sight, the man now looked very weak from hunger and cold. Pip half expected him to drop down dead, but he grabbed the bag of food and started tearing it apart in desperation and gratitude. He ate the whole pork pie greedily, washing it down with a great gulp of brandy.

'I'm Magwitch,' he belched as he began to file through his leg iron.

'I'm Pip,' replied Pip. 'I'm glad you enjoyed the food.'

'Thank'ee, my boy. I did. Happy Christmas.'

When he was very young, Philip Pirrip hadn't been able to get his mouth round his real name. The best he could manage was 'Pip', and ever since then everyone had just called him Pip. After his parents died, Pip had lived

with his good-natured, sweet-tempered uncle,
Joe Gargery, who was the village blacksmith.
Joe had the misfortune of being married to
Pip's older sister, the ill-natured, bad-tempered
Mrs Joe.

'Ever the best of friends, ain't we Pip old
chap?' smiled Joe as Pip warmed himself by
the fire. 'Where 'ave you been so early in the
morning? You'll do yourself a mischief.'

Mrs Joe stormed into the room, as angry as ever with Pip. 'You should be more grateful to your sister who has brought you up by hand,' she scowled. 'I don't know why I said I'd take you in. It's a hard, thankless job. Going out in the cold and damp on Christmas morning! You should be more grateful.'

Pip tried very hard to look grateful, but it had no effect upon her.

'Did you hear the gun sound last night, Pip old chap?' asked Joe. 'It means a prisoner has escaped from the prison ships. An escaped convict is out there somewhere, old chap. It was dangerous for you to go out.'

Pip thought of the man in the leg iron, so hungry and cold. 'Who is in those ships?' he asked. 'What is it that they have done wrong?'

This enraged Mrs Joe even more. 'I didn't bring you up by hand just so you could bother me with questions. They're there because they murder and rob and cheat, and because they

ask too many questions. You should be more grateful to your sister who brought you up by h—.'

Her tirade was cut short by a firm knock on the door. Pip held his breath.

Mrs Joe went into the kitchen, and Joe opened the door to a group of uniformed soldiers. Pip trembled; he knew that the soldiers had come for him, the ungrateful boy who stole pork pies and asked too many questions.

Mrs Joe ran in from the kitchen. 'My pork pie is gone!' she screamed. It suddenly crossed Pip's mind that he might be safer with the soldiers than with his sister.

The soldiers searched and questioned, questioned and searched. Piecing the evidence together, the soldiers' captain grandly announced, 'It seems the escaped convict 'as been 'ere and 'as stolen your pork pie.' They asked Joe and Pip to help them search the

marshes for the dangerous
convict and the missing
pork pie.

In the cold morning light
the search party easily found
Magwitch, hiding in a ditch. In
all the splashing and swearing
of the struggle Magwitch didn't
once look at Pip. 'I nearly died

last night,' he shouted. 'If it 'adn't been for a pork pie ...' – Pip held his breath – '... wot I stole from a blacksmith's 'ouse, I'd be a dead man. Stealing that pork pie saved me life.'

As Magwitch was led away, Pip felt that his own life had been saved by the convict's lie. Joe put a warm arm round Pip's shoulders and led him home.

Joe Gargery's Uncle Pumblechook was a boastful, unpleasant man, with a mouth like a fish and dull, staring eyes. He had brought a bottle of wine to Christmas dinner at the Gargerys', and was happily drinking it all himself.

'There's nothing worse than an ungrateful boy,' he preached to the assembled company. Then he looked pointedly at Pip: 'You should be more grateful to them what brought you up by 'and.'

Joe poured Pip some extra gravy.

'Now boy,' continued Pumblechook, 'if you ain't grateful this night, you never will be.' He puffed out his chest like a proud rooster. 'Your Uncle Pumblechook 'as used 'is very considerable influence on your be'alf. You will 'ave 'eard of the wealthy, grand Miss Havisham what lives in the big 'ouse. You are to 'ave the honour of going to play with 'er niece. Now you show your gratitude to them who 'elps you, boy.'

Again Pip tried very hard to look as grateful as possible. Inside his little body, however, his heart sank.

'God bless you, Pip old chap,' whispered Joe, and poured him yet more gravy.

Great preparations were made for Pip's first
visit to Miss Havisham's. He was soaped
and scrubbed and kneaded and soaked and
towelled and rubbed and rasped until his skin
was pink and shiny. Dressed in uncomfortably
tight clothes, Pip felt very nervous as Uncle
Pumblechook's coach drew up outside the gates
of the big house.

Pip stepped down timidly. He was greeted by a girl of about his own age, who would have been beautiful if she had had any warmth and friendliness in her face, but she had only coldness and scorn. Though Pip's age, the girl seemed more like a young lady. 'Come this way, boy,' she commanded.

The young lady led Pip along a cold, sunless corridor, at the end of which was a door upon which she knocked.

'Who is it?'

'It is Estella. I have brought the boy.'

The door creaked open. Stepping into the room, Pip was surprised that it was almost as dark as the corridor had been. Nevertheless, he could see well enough to behold a very strange sight indeed.

Miss Havisham, like a ghost, was a vision of paleness. She wore a long, faded white dress of satin and lace, with white shoes of the same material. Her skin and hair had faded almost to white, and from her white hair hung a faded white veil. Even the flowers in her hair, which must once have been so colourful, had faded to colourless white. The only relief amidst all this lost beauty was provided by her sparkling diamond necklace.

Pip was told to sit down to play cards with Estella, who immediately took charge of the game. She explained the rules so quickly that Pip hardly had time to think. Miss Havisham watched the pair with satisfaction.

Pip suspected that the curtains had never been opened to let the sunlight in. A layer of dust covered every surface. On a table Pip saw what could only be a wedding cake, complete and uncut, covered in dust. Through the dust-filled air Pip could see two clocks; both had stopped at exactly the same time, twenty minutes to nine. Time stood still in this gloomy room as dust continued to settle on dust.

When Pip made a mistake and picked up the wrong card, Estella rolled her eyes. 'What a stupid clumsy boy you are!' she sneered, 'and what very coarse hands you have.' Pip said nothing, but he was not enjoying himself.

At the end of the game Miss Havisham drew Pip to her. 'I hear what Estella thinks of you,' she said, 'but what do *you* think of *her*, Pip?'

'I d—do not like to say,' Pip stammered.

'Then tell me in my ear.'

Pip whispered, 'I think she is very proud. I think she is very pretty. I think she is very insulting. I should like to go home.'

Pip's visits to Miss Havisham's house became a regular occurrence, always following a similar pattern. 'Play, play, play!' commanded the ghastly, ghostly lady, and Pip always obeyed, though the strangeness of the room still distracted him.

Pip learned that, many years ago, the man that Miss Havisham was to marry cancelled the wedding the very day it was to take place. The wedding day had come, but not the groom. Since that dreadful day neither the heartbroken bride nor her room had changed, other than gently fading and gathering dust.

'Look at me,' she once asked Pip, putting her hand to her breast. 'What do I touch?'

'Your heart, Miss Havisham?'

'Broken, Pip, broken.' She turned to Estella. 'If you can break Pip's heart as mine is broken,' she told her, 'then break it. Have no mercy.'

Pip did not play his cards very well that morning.

As she walked him back to the gates, Estella remained cold and contemptuous, looking at him as if he were a dog in disgrace. Pip felt humiliated, hurt and angry. When tears started to sting his eyes Estella glanced at him

with delight. 'You may kiss me if you like, boy,'
she said.

Pip kissed her cold cheek, but vowed that
he would never cry for her again.

In the smithy Joe was skilfully hammering red-hot iron into a horseshoe. Pip studied Joe's hard-working hands, then looked at his own. 'I wish I wasn't so common,' complained Pip.

'You must be content to live well and die happy,' responded Joe.

Pip looked away. 'But I want to be a gentleman,' he thought to himself. 'I want Estella to admire me.'

With this goal in mind, Pip set himself to learn reading and writing. His friend Biddy agreed to help him. Like Pip, Biddy was an orphan who was expected to be grateful. Her hair was untidy, her hands dirty, her shoes broken, but she was always happy and obliging. With Biddy's help, Pip made rapid progress.

'Why didn't you ever go to school?' Pip asked Joe one evening.

'My father wouldn't let me, old chap. It were quite a drawback on me learning.'

Pip wrote the word 'Joe' on a piece of paper. 'Can you read this, Joe?'

'Well, there's a J, and I think an O,' studied Joe. 'Why, it says Joe! How astonishing reading is! You *are* a scholar, Pip.'

The shame Pip felt in relation to Joe reached a new height when Miss Havisham asked Joe to visit her. Poor Joe was anxious and uncomfortable in his Sunday suit.

'You are the husband of the sister of this boy?' inquired the grand, fading bride.

'Ever the best of friends, ain't we, Pip old chap?' smiled Joe. Pip looked down at Joe's rough hands, fidgeting nervously at his sides.

'And you have the intention of making him your apprentice?'

'It is the first wish of 'is 'eart, isn't it, old chap?'

Pip squirmed with embarrassment, wishing that Joe would direct his answers to the person asking the questions, rather than to him. He noticed Estella smirking.

'Then I shall pay for his apprenticeship,' said Miss Havisham. 'He has been a good boy, and this is his reward.'

So Pip began working as Joe's apprentice, and his visits to Miss Havisham's house ceased. Though he no longer saw Estella, he still burned with the shame she had kindled within him. Becoming a blacksmith was no longer the first wish of his heart, and he resented his time with Joe.

Three years passed. Pip grew into a young man, Mrs Joe became seriously ill, and Biddy moved into their household to look after her.

Biddy became Pip's true friend and confidante. 'I wish I could make myself fall in love with you instead of with Estella,' Pip told her one day, 'but I want to be a gentleman. I feel ashamed of my life here.'

Biddy replied quietly. 'This plain, honest, working life to which you have been born is nothing to be ashamed of.'

'Joe is a good fellow,' said Pip, 'just a little backward in his learning and his manners.'

Biddy said nothing.

Sitting beside Joe during one of their evening
visits to The Three Jolly Bargemen, Pip
glanced up from his drink and noticed a
smartly-dressed man looking directly at him.
Though it happened very quickly, Pip was
certain that the man held up briefly the file
that Pip had stolen for the convict all those
years ago. Swiftly returning it to his pocket,
the man beckoned Pip and Joe to follow him
outside.

'My name is Jaggars. I am a London lawyer.
I have a matter of profound importance for
you.' Joe put his arm protectively around Pip's
shoulders. 'Someone, and I can't say who,
wishes to make Pip wealthy. Pip will shortly
be taken to London to be brought up as a
gentleman. He has great expectations.'

Preparations for Pip's departure were made
swiftly. Pip was very excited, Joe and Biddy

sad and quiet. Pip knew in his heart that Miss
Havisham was responsible for this change in
his fortunes. She was going to make him a
gentleman so he would be worthy of Estella.
He completely forgot to wonder why, and how,
Mr Jaggars had shown him the file.

Joe wept when Pip left, and Biddy covered
her face with her apron. Proudly refusing Joe's
offer to accompany him on the journey, Pip
fought back the sobs rising in his throat and
turned to face London alone.

Everything was arranged. Jaggars became Pip's guardian. Pip was tutored by the kindly Mr Pocket, and moved into lodgings with Mr Pocket's son Herbert. Pip was not allowed to ask questions about his fortune or his benefactor; his only duty was to become a gentleman.

Herbert Pocket was a pale young man, with an easy manner and high spirits. Living, studying and relaxing together every day, Pip and Herbert became great friends.

The busy streets of London became Pip's new home. He spent his money carelessly and enjoyed the pleasures of the city in his efforts to become worthy of Estella. He rarely thought of his old home in the marshes, and of Joe, Mrs Joe and Biddy.

It was with mixed feelings that Pip read a letter from Biddy telling him that Joe would like to

visit him in London. Pip felt awkward about introducing his urbane friend Herbert to his blacksmith uncle.

Joe was just as uneasy with Herbert as he had been with Miss Havisham. Pip was particularly embarrassed when Joe exclaimed ''Ow you have growed, sir! You are an honour to your king and country.' Herbert excused himself and went to make tea. Joe took the opportunity to explain the reason for his visit. 'Miss 'avisham sends you a message, Pip sir. Miss Estella would be glad to see you if you would visit.'

Pip noticed that Joe finished his tea as quickly as possible, then stood up to leave.

'You're not going so soon, are you?' said Pip, surprised. 'Are you not staying for dinner?'

'No sir – Pip, me old chap. Life is made of many goodbyes, and I won't be visiting you in London again. It ain't that I'm proud, but I'm wrong 'ere with you. I'm wrong away from me workshop and the marshes. You find fault with me 'ere that you wouldn't if we were at 'ome together. I'm awful dull at learning, but I 'ope I'm a good man and a good blacksmith. God bless you, Pip old chap.' Gently kissing Pip on the cheek, Joe picked up his hat and left.

Pip was speechless. He rushed out, but Joe had already disappeared into London's crowded streets.

Pip followed Miss Havisham's instructions
and took a coach the next day. He thought
about staying with Joe, but instead decided
that a gentleman would take a room in an
inn. Pip was sure that Miss Havisham had
summoned him to marry Estella. After such
a long absence Pip was eager to see her,

and present himself at last as a true gentleman.

'Is she not more beautiful than ever?' asked Miss Havisham when they all met again.

'Indeed she is.'

'And what about him?' she asked Estella. 'Is he still coarse and common?'

Estella laughed, but later, when the two were alone together, she confided in him: 'You should know, Pip, that I have no heart. I have no warmth in me, no sympathy, no love.'

When Pip came to bid Miss Havisham farewell, she dug her bony fingers into his arm. 'Love her, love her, love her,' she insisted. I have made her what she is so that she will break men's hearts just as a man once broke mine. You must give your heart and soul to her!'

In a state of shock, Pip left the house as fast as politeness and his feet would allow.

He was now very confused, and that night in the inn he could not sleep, saying to himself over and over again, 'But I do love her, I do love her!' In his confusion both Joe and his sick wife were forgotten. As Pip took the first coach back to London, he did not know that he had missed the last chance to see his sister alive.

Pip threw himself back into his London life with renewed energy and extravagance, but the more the money flowed the more miserable he seemed to grow. One day a letter arrived with an ominous black seal. It informed Pip that Mrs Joe Gargery had departed this life, and that Pip's attendance was requested at the funeral the following Monday afternoon.

Joe welcomed Pip back into his home with open arms. Warming themselves together by the fire, Pip felt the pride that had frosted his heart slowly melting away as Joe told him all about Mrs Joe's illness and asked him all about his life in London.

Biddy, too, welcomed Pip warmly. He felt ashamed of the way he had treated these good people. Biddy, however, being wiser than Pip, knew that London and Estella would soon occupy his thoughts and his heart again.

Since his last strange visit to Miss Havisham's, Pip had begun to doubt that she could be his benefactor. He decided to visit her before returning to London.

Miss Havisham had aged, and the wedding dress now hung loosely around her skeletal figure. Though more layers of dust had settled, the clocks still stood at twenty minutes to nine.

Estella, still beautiful but for the coldness of her smile, sat in her usual place by Miss Havisham's side.

'Miss Havisham,' began Pip, 'in apprenticing me to Joe you had already rewarded me most generously. I must now ask you whether it was also you that positioned me in London and gave me my great expectations.'

'That was not I.'

Pip's mind raced. Who then was his benefactor? If Miss Havisham had not done this to prepare him for Estella, what was now to be done? He summoned up his courage.

'In an attempt to ease the pain of your own broken heart you encouraged Estella to break mine. Was that kind?'

Miss Havisham again put her hand to her heart and held it there, but it was Estella who spoke. 'It seems that you ignored my warnings,' she said calmly. 'I have only ice where my heart should be. I cannot love.'

Miss Havisham had sunk deeply into her chair. In a frail voice she said, 'But Estella, you love me, don't you, child? I want you to love *me*.'

'I am what you have made me,' answered Estella. 'It is you that stole my heart and put ice in its place.' She stood up, glanced sadly yet softly at Pip, and left the room.

As Pip left Miss Havisham's house two questions burned in his mind. Who then *was* his benefactor, and how could he ever thaw the ice of Estella's cold, cold heart? He looked back at the window of the dusty room where he thought he had said his final farewell to Miss Havisham. What he saw made him turn and run back. Taking the stairs two at a time, he darted along the dark corridor and crashed through Miss Havisham's locked door.

She ran at him, shrieking, fire burning all about her. No longer a place of ice-cold

faded white, the room was ablaze with a fury of orange and red. Pip tore off his coat and flung Miss Havisham to the ground. He wrapped her; he rolled her. Ablaze, they struggled like desperate enemies. She shrieked, fighting to free herself, but Pip held her tight until the flames, and she, had spent their fury.

'Forgive me,' she whispered through dying lips. 'Forgive me.'

'I forgive you,' groaned Pip.

Badly burned himself, Pip needed constant care when he returned to London. Joe left the marshes to share the nursing with Herbert.

Pip's heart ached to think of his ingratitude to his generous uncle. 'Please don't be so good to me,' he told Joe. 'Please look angry with me!'

'Ever the best of friends, old chap,'

replied Joe, tenderly changing the dressing
on Pip's arm.

During the following weeks Pip received many
visitors. One evening he opened the door to a
man with long grey hair. His skin was brown
and hardened by exposure to the weather.

He put a small parcel on the table. 'Open it.'

Pip cautiously opened the parcel. It was a pork pie. 'My convict!' he exclaimed.

'Aye,' grinned Magwitch. 'You acted nobly that day, my boy, and I 'ave not forgot it.' Pip suddenly felt the fear that he had felt as a boy that Christmas day in the marshes. Magwitch had noticed. 'Don't be afraid. I mean you no 'arm.'

Now Pip also remembered the evening in The Three Jolly Bargemen when Jaggars had briefly held up the file. 'D—d—do you know Mr Jaggars?' he asked, dreading the answer.

'Indeed I do, my boy. I knowed as you wanted to be a gentleman; it is me wot 'as done it.'

Joy glowed in the old villain's face, while horror drained the colour from Pip's. All his wealth had come from this criminal's money. In thinking himself so grand all these years,

Pip had betrayed Joe's love in favour of this rough convict.

Magwitch interpreted Pip's horror as amazement. 'It 'as been my pleasure,' he smiled. 'I 'ave worked hard all these years and made me fortune overseas just to make you a gentleman. You are my gentleman.'

Out of politeness more than gratitude,

Pip invited Magwitch to share a pot of tea. Magwitch told him how, following his arrest on the marshes, he had been transported to the prisoners' colony in Australia. Never forgetting the little boy who had saved his life, he had worked hard to create a fortune through cattle trading. He had sent money to Jaggars with strict instructions that Pip should not know where it came from. Now he had come home to reunite himself with his gentleman.

'Of course, it's death for me if I am caught,' he explained.

'Then surely you must return to Australia.'

'Oh no, I am not going back! I've come 'ome for good. I need you to 'elp me stay 'idden.'

Pip found Magwitch secret lodgings by the River Thames. He visited regularly, and grew fond of the generous old rogue. A couple of months later Pip found a new and safer hiding place further up-river, but as he rowed Magwitch up the Thames towards his new home they were intercepted by the police. Just as so long ago on the marshes, Magwitch was taken away. Just as on the marshes, Pip watched with a mixture of horror and relief.

Ever cunning in escaping the law, Magwitch found a way of escaping the hangman's noose. He grew seriously ill in prison. With his head cradled in Pip's arms he died a peaceful, natural death. He smiled as he uttered his last words. 'My gentleman, Pip, my gentleman.'

Pip's fountain of wealth dried up with Magwitch's passing. Full of love, ashamed and apologetic, he returned to his old home on the marshes.

He found Biddy, all smiles, arm in arm with Joe.
Bursting with happiness, she ran to Pip. 'Pip!'
she laughed. 'It is my wedding day. I am married
to Joe.' Joe too was all smiles. 'Pip, old chap,
welcome 'ome!' The fire in the old hearth glowed
a warm welcome.

Years later, during one of his regular trips to
his old family home, an older Pip wandered
around the grounds of Miss Havisham's house.
The neglected walls were crumbling, and weeds
covered the courtyard. The upstairs window
was still blackened by the fatal fire. Sitting on
a broken wall, lost in a world of memories, Pip
was surprised to hear the soft sound of a footfall.
Turning, he thought he saw Estella walking
towards him. He blinked. It *was* Estella. She
looked older, but she was still beautiful.

'Pip, I hardly recognised you,' she gasped.

'I should always recognise you,' replied Pip.

Like Pip, this was the first time Estella had visited the house for many years. Since they had last met, life had greatly changed for them both. Estella accepted Pip's invitation to visit him at Joe and Biddy's home.

The next day, Estella sat smiling with warmth and mature beauty before Joe's roaring fire. The warm glow reflected in her bright eyes as she allowed Pip to hold her smooth hand in his. When Biddy and Joe went into the kitchen, Estella leaned over and said quietly to Pip, 'I do believe the ice around my heart is beginning to thaw.'

TAKING THINGS FURTHER

The real read

This *Real Read* version of *Great Expectations* is a retelling of Charles Dickens' magnificent work. If you would like to read the full novel in all its original splendour, many complete editions are available, from bargain paperbacks to beautifully bound hardbacks. You may well find a copy in your local charity shop.

Filling in the spaces

The loss of so many of Charles Dickens' original words is a sad but necessary part of the shortening process. We have had to make some difficult decisions, omitting subplots and details, some important, some less so, but all interesting. We have also, at times, taken the liberty of combining two events into one, or of giving a character words or actions that originally belong to another. The points below will fill in some of the gaps, but nothing can beat the original.

- There is another convict on the marshes on Christmas Day. His name is Compeyson. He and Magwitch were once associates in crime, Magwitch being subservient to Compeyson.

- At the end of the novel, Compeyson is responsible for reporting Magwitch's whereabouts to the police. Magwitch and Compeyson fight in the Thames. Compeyson drowns and Magwitch sustains injuries which lead to his own illness and eventual death in prison.

- Compeyson is also the man who broke Miss Havisham's heart as part of a confidence trick to gain money from her.

- Estella is not related to Miss Havisham, but is adopted. Years ago, Jaggers, the lawyer, helped to defend a woman called Molly who was accused of murder. At the time, Molly had an illegitimate baby, Estella. When Miss Havisham's heart was broken by Compeyson, she asked Jaggers to find a child for her to adopt. Jaggers brought her Estella. Estella's mother Molly is now Jaggers' housekeeper.

- Pip discovers that Magwitch is Estella's father. Magwitch had loved the baby, but didn't know what had happened to her after Molly's trial. As Magwitch dies, Pip says to him, 'You had a child once whom you loved and lost. She lived and found powerful friends. She is living now. She is a lady and is very beautiful. And I love her.' This revelation, and Magwitch's response, makes his death very moving.

- Herbert Pocket is a relative of Miss Havisham. Pip had already met him once, when they were boys, on a visit to Miss Havisham's.

- Herbert's fortune is not as great as Pip's. Their extravagant living in London leads Herbert into debt. Pip realises that he must bear some responsibility, and decides to make amends. He visits Jaggers and arranges to make regular payments to Herbert from his own wealth, but anonymously. Pip also persuades

Miss Havisham of Herbert's good character, and she leaves him money in her will.

- When Pip's fortune disappears with Magwitch's death, he goes abroad to work for Herbert for eleven years. His meeting with Estella in the grounds of Miss Havisham's ruined house takes place after this period of time.

- Between Miss Havisham's fire and the end of the novel, Estella marries an unpleasant man called Drummle. Their marriage is very unhappy. When she finally meets Pip, she is a widow.

- Mrs Joe's illness and death are actually due to her having been attacked by Joe's bitter, jealous employee Orlick. Orlick also attacks and almost kills Pip, who is saved by Herbert.

Back in time

Victorian England was experiencing a period of great transition. Having been an agricultural, rural economy, it was moving swiftly towards industrial nationhood. The old rural life, represented in *Great Expectations* by Joe, was being lost as people aspired to greater wealth. Like Pip, many left traditional rural life in favour of cities like London.

A new 'middle class' was emerging. These people were below the aristocracy, their wealth usually created through trade and industry. This gave rise to a lively debate about the nature of a true gentleman. To be considered a gentleman required a combination of wealth, education and manners. Pip spends much of his time in London studying to acquire the education to be considered a gentleman.

The Victorians believed that they could overcome crime. Great numbers of prisoners were transported to colonies in Australia. This practice peaked between 1820 and 1850.

Charles Dickens experienced poverty at first hand – his father was imprisoned for debt and the young Charles made to work in a warehouse. These experiences affected him deeply.

Finding out more

We recommend the following books and websites to gain a greater understanding of Charles Dickens' and Pip's England:

Books

- Terry Deary, *Loathsome London* (Horrible Histories), Scholastic, 2005.

- Terry Deary, *Vile Victorians* (Horrible Histories), Scholastic, 1994.

- *Victorian London*, Watling Street Publishing, 2005.

- Ann Kramer, *Victorians* (Eyewitness Guides), Dorling Kindersley, 1998.

- Peter Ackroyd, *Dickens*, BBC, 2003.

Websites

- www.victorianweb.org
Scholarly information on all aspects of
Victorian life, including literature, history and
culture.

- www.bbc.co.uk/history/british/victorians
The BBC's interactive site about Victorian
Britain, with a wide range of information and
activities for all ages.

- www.dickensmuseum.com
Home of the Dickens Museum in London,
with details about exhibits, events and lots of
helpful links.

- www.dickensworld.co.uk
Dickens World, based in Chatham in Kent, is
a themed visitor complex featuring the life,
books and times of Charles Dickens.

- www.charlesdickenspage.com
A labour of love dedicated to Dickens, with
information about his life and his novels.
Many useful links.

Food for thought

Here are some things to think about if you are reading *Great Expectations* alone, or ideas for discussion if you are reading it with friends.

In retelling *Great Expectations* we have tried to recreate, as accurately as possible, Dickens' original plot and characters. We have also tried to imitate aspects of his style. Remember, however, that this is not the original work; thinking about the points below, therefore, can help you begin to understand Charles Dickens' craft. To move forward from here, turn to the full-length version of *Great Expectations* and lose yourself in his wonderful storytelling.

Starting points

- Which character interests you the most? Why?

- How do you feel about Pip's treatment of Joe?

- What do you think about Miss Havisham's and Estella's behaviour towards Pip?

- How surprised were you to discover the truth about Pip's benefactor? Had there been any clues in the story?

- Which aspects of Pip's character do you like or dislike?

Themes

What do you think Charles Dickens is saying about the following themes in *Great Expectations*?

- loyalty
- pride
- gratitude
- love
- what it means to be a gentleman

Style

Can you find paragraphs containing examples of the following?

- descriptions of setting and atmosphere
- the use of repetition to enhance description
- different characters speaking in different ways
- the use of imagery to enhance description

Look closely at how these paragraphs are written. What do you notice? Can you write a paragraph in the same style?

Symbols

Writers frequently use symbols in their work to deepen the reader's emotions and understanding. Charles Dickens is no exception. Think about how the symbols in this list match the action in *Great Expectations*.

- the pork pie
- hands
- fire
- ice